W9-CDC-061

DISCARDED

THE CELEBRATED

JUMPING FROG OF CALAVERAS COUNTY

MARK TWAIN

CREATIVE EDUCATION INC.

Published by Creative Education, Inc.
123 S. Broad Street, Mankato, Minnesota 56001

Designed by Rita Marshall
Cover Illustration by Etienne Delessert

Library of Congress Cataloging-in-Publication Data

Twain, Mark, 1835–1910.
    The celebrated jumping frog of Calaveras County/by Mark Twain.
    p.   cm.
    Summary: A man who loves to place bets acquires a remarkable
frog which he claims can outjump any other frog in the county.
    ISBN 0-88682-296-3
    [1. Frogs—Fiction.   2. Contests—Fiction.]   I. Title.
PZ7.C584Ce   1989
[Fic]—dc20   89-37307
                                                        CIP
                                                        AC

To THE CONTINUATION

OF FINE LITERATURE FOR

READERS OF ALL AGES.

IN COMPLIANCE WITH THE REQUEST OF A

FRIEND OF MINE, WHO WROTE ME FROM

the East, I called on good-natured, garrulous old

Simon Wheeler, and inquired after my friend's

friend, Leonidas W. *Smiley, as requested to do,*

and I hereunto append the result. I have a

lurking suspicion that Leonidas W. *Smiley is a*

myth; that my friend never knew such a

personage; and that he only conjectured that, if

I asked old Wheeler about him, it would

remind him of his infamous Jim *Smiley, and he*

would go to work and bore me nearly to death

with some exasperating reminiscence of him as

long and tedious as it should be useless to me. If

that was the design, it succeeded.

I found Simon Wheeler dozing comfortably by the bar-room stove of the dilapidated tavern in the decayed mining camp of Angel's, and I noticed that he was fat and bald-headed, and had an expression of winning gentleness and simplicity upon his tranquil countenance. He roused up and gave me good-day. I told him a friend of mine had commissioned me to make some inquiries about a cherished companion of his boyhood named *Leonidas W.* Smiley—*Rev. Leonidas W.* Smiley—a young minister of the Gospel, who he had heard was at one time a resident of Angel's Camp. I added that, if Mr.

Wheeler could tell me anything about this Rev. Leonidas W. Smiley, I would feel under many obligations to him.

Simon Wheeler backed me into a corner and blockaded me there with his chair, and then sat me down and reeled off the monotonous narrative which follows this paragraph. He never smiled, he never frowned, he never changed his voice from the gentle-flowing key to which he tuned the initial sentence, he never betrayed the slightest suspicion of enthusiasm; but all through the interminable narrative there ran a vein of impressive earnestness and sincerity, which showed me plainly

that, so far from his imagining that there was

anything ridiculous or funny about his story, he

regarded it as a really important matter, and

admired its two heroes as men of transcendent

genius in *finesse.* I let him go on in his own way,

and never interrupted him once:

"Rev. Leonidas W. H'm, Reverend Le—well,

there was a feller here once by the name of *Jim*

Smiley, in the winter of '49—or maybe it was

the spring of '50—I don't recollect exactly,

somehow, though what makes me think it was

one or the other is because I remember the big

flume wasn't finished when he first came to the camp; but any way, he was the curiousest man about always betting on any thing that turned up you ever see, if he could get any body to bet on the other side; and if he couldn't, he'd change sides. Any way that suited the other man would suit him—any way just so's he got a bet, *he* was satisfied. But still he was lucky, uncommon lucky; he most always come out winner. He was always ready and laying for a chance; there couldn't be no solit'ry thing mentioned but that feller'd offer to bet on it, and take any side you please, as I was just telling you. If there was a horse-race, you'd find him flush, or you'd find him busted at the end of it; if there was a dog-fight, he'd bet on it; if there was a cat-fight, he'd bet on it; if there was a chicken-fight, he'd bet on it; why, if there was two birds setting on a fence, he would bet you which one would fly first; or if there was a camp-meeting, he would be there reg'lar, to bet on Parson Walker, which he judged to be the best exhorter about there, and so he was, too, and a good man. If he even seen a straddle-bug start to go any-wheres, he would bet you how long it would take him to get wherever he was going to, and

if you took him up, he would foller that straddle-bug to Mexico but what he would find out
where he was bound for and how long he was
on the road. Lots of the boys here has seen that
Smiley, and can tell you about him. Why, it
never made no difference to *him*—he would
bet on *any* thing—the dangdest feller. Parson
Walker's wife laid very sick once, for a good
while, and it seemed as if they warn't going to
save her; but one morning he come in, and Smiley asked how she was, and he said she was
considerable better—thank the Lord for his
inf'nite mercy—and coming on so smart that,

with the blessing of Prov'dence, she'd get well yet; and Smiley, before he thought, says, "Well, I'll resk two-and-a-half that she don't, anyway."

Thish-yer Smiley had a mare—the boys called her the fifteen-minute nag, but that was only in fun, you know, because, of course, she was faster than that—and he used to win money on that horse, for all she was so slow and always had the asthma, or the distemper, or the consumption, or something of that kind. They used to give her two or three hundred yards start, and then pass her under way; but always at the fag-end of the race she'd get excited and

desperate-like, and come cavorting and strad-
dling up, and scattering her legs around limber,
sometimes in the air, and sometimes out to one
side amongst the fences, and kicking up
m-o-r-e dust, and raising m-o-r-e racket with
her coughing and sneezing and blowing her
nose—and always fetch up at the stand just
about a neck ahead, as near as you could cipher
it down.

And he had a little small bull pup, that to
look at him you'd think he wa'nt worth a cent,
but to set around and look ornery, and lay for a
chance to steal something. But as soon as

money was up on him, he was a different dog;

his under-jaw'd begin to stick out like the

fo'castle of a steamboat, and his teeth would

uncover, and shine savage like the furnaces.

And a dog might tackle him, and bully-rag him,

and bite him, and throw him over his shoulder

two or three times, and Andrew Jackson—

which was the name of the pup—Andrew Jack-

son would never let on but what *he* was satis-

fied, and hadn't expected nothing else—and

the bets being doubled and doubled on the

other side all the time, till the money was all up;

and then all of a sudden he would grab that

other dog jest by the j'int of his hind leg and freeze to it—not chaw, you understand, but only jest grip and hang on till they throwed up the sponge, if it was a year. Smiley always come out winner on that pup, till he harnessed a dog once that didn't have no hind legs, because they'd been sawed off by a circular saw, and when the thing had gone along far enough, and the money was all up, and he come to make a snatch for his pet holt, he saw in a minute how he'd been imposed on, and how the other dog had him in the door, so to speak, and he 'peared surprised, and then he looked sorter discouraged-like, and didn't try no more to win the fight, and so he got shucked out bad. He give Smiley a look, as much as to say his heart was broke, and it was *his* fault, for putting up a dog that hadn't no hind legs for him to take holt of, which was his main dependence in a fight, and then he limped off a piece and laid down and died. It was a good pup, was that Andrew Jackson, and would have made a name for hisself if he'd lived, for the stuff was in him, and he had genius—I know it, because he hadn't had no opportunities to speak of, and it don't stand to reason that a dog could make such a fight as he

could under them circumstances, if he hadn't
no talent. It always makes me feel sorry when I
think of that last fight of his'n, and the way it
turned out.

Well, thish-yer Smiley had rat-tarriers, and
chicken cocks, and tom-cats, and all them kind
of things, till you couldn't rest, and you
couldn't fetch nothing for him to bet on but
he'd match you. He ketched a frog one day, and
took him home, and said he calk'lated to eder-
cate him; and so he never done nothing for
three months but set in his back yard and learn
that frog to jump. And you bet he *did* learn him,

too. He'd give him a little punch behind, and the next minute you'd see that frog whirling in the air like a doughnut—see him turn one summerset, or may be a couple, if he got a good start, and come down flat-footed and all right, like a cat. He got him up so in the matter of catching flies, and kept him in practice so constant, that he'd nail a fly every time as far as he could see him. Smiley said all a frog wanted was education, and he could do most anything— and I believe him. Why, I've seen him set Dan'l Webster down here on this floor—Dan'l Webster was the name of the frog—and sing out,

"Flies, Dan'l, flies!" and quicker'n you could wink, he'd spring straight up, and snake a fly off'n the counter there, and flop down on the floor again as solid as a gob of mud, and fall to scratching the side of his head with his hind foot as indifferent as if he hadn't no idea he'd been doin' any more'n any frog might do. You never see a frog so modest and straightfor'ard as he was, for all he was so gifted. And when it come to fair and square jumping on a dead level, he could get over more ground at one straddle than any animal of his breed you ever see. Jumping on a dead level was his strong suit, you understand; and when it come to that, Smiley would ante up money on him as long as he had a red. Smiley was monstrous proud of his frog, and well he might be, for fellers that had been everywheres, all said he laid over any frog that ever *they* see.

Well, Smiley kept the beast in a little lattice box, and he used to fetch him down town sometimes and lay for a bet. One day a feller—a stranger in the camp, he was—come across him with his box, and says:

"What might it be that you've got in that box?"

And Smiley says, sorter indifferent like, "It might be a parrot, or it might be a canary, may be, but it ain't—it's only a frog."

And the feller took it, and looked at it careful, and turned it round this way and that, and says, "H'm—so 'tis. Well, what's *he* good for?"

"Well," Smiley says, easy and careless, "he's good enough for *one* thing, I should judge—he can outjump any frog in Calaveras county."

The feller took the box again, and took another long, particular look, and give it back to Smiley, and says, very deliberate, "Well, I don't see no p'ints about that frog that's any better'n any other frog."

"May be you don't," Smiley says. "May be you understand frogs, and maybe you don't understand 'em; may be you've had experience, and may be you ain't only a amature, as it were. Anyways I've got *my* opinion, and I'll risk forty dollars he can outjump any frog in Calaveras county."

And the feller studied a minute, and then says, kinder sad like, "Well, I'm only a stranger here, and I ain't got no frog; but if I had a frog, I'd bet you."

And then Smiley says, "That's all right—that's

all right—if you'll hold my box a minute, I'll go and get you a frog." And so the feller took the box, and put up his forty dollars along with Smiley's, and set down to wait.

So he set there a good while thinking and thinking to hisself, and then he got the frog out and prized his mouth open and took a teaspoon and filled him full of quail shot—filled him pretty near up to his chin—and set him on the floor. Smiley he went to the swamp and slopped around in the mud for a long time, and finally he ketched a frog, and fetched it in, and give him to this feller, and says:

"Now, if you're ready, set him along side of Dan'l, with his fore-paws just even with Dan'l, and I'll give the word." Then he says, "One—two—three—jump!" and him and the feller touched up the frogs from behind, and the new frog hopped off, but Dan'l give a heave, and hysted up his shoulders—so—like a Frenchman, but it wan't no use—he couldn't budge; he was planted as solid as an anvil, and he couldn't no more stir than if he was anchored out. Smiley was a good deal surprised, and he was disgusted too, but he didn't have no idea what the matter was, of course.

The feller took the money and started away;
and when he was going out at the door, he
sorter jerked his thumb over his shoulders—
this way—at Dan'l, and says again, very deliberate, "Well, *I* don't see no p'ints about that
frog that's any better'n any other frog."

Smiley he stood scratching his head and look-
ing down at Dan'l a long time, and at last he
says, "I do wonder what in the nation that frog
throw'd off for—I wonder if there ain't something the matter with him—he 'pears to look
mighty baggy, somehow." And he ketched
Dan'l by the nap of the neck, and lifted him up

and says, "Why, blame my cats, if he don't weigh five pound!" and turned him upside down, and he belched out a double handful of shot. And then he see how it was, and he was the maddest man—he set the frog down and took out after that feller, but he never ketched him. And—

(Here Simon Wheeler heard his name called from the front yard, and got up to see what was wanted.) And turning to me as he moved away, he said: "Just set where you are, stranger, and rest easy—I ain't going to be gone a second."

But, by your leave, I did not think that a

continuation of the history of the enterprising vagabond *Jim* Smiley would be likely to afford me much information concerning the Rev. *Leonidas W.* Smiley, and so I started away.

At the door I met the sociable Wheeler returning, and he buttonholed me and recommenced:

"Well, thish-yer Smiley had a yeller one-eyed cow that didn't have no tail, only jest a short stump like a bannanner, and—"

"Oh! hang Smiley and his afflicted cow!" I muttered, good-naturedly, and bidding the old gentleman good-day, I departed.